J B Domino
DeMocker, Michael,
Fats Domino /
$29.95   on1107492640

3 4028 09979 3359
HARRIS COUNTY PUBLIC LIBRARY

WITHDRAWN

D1452135

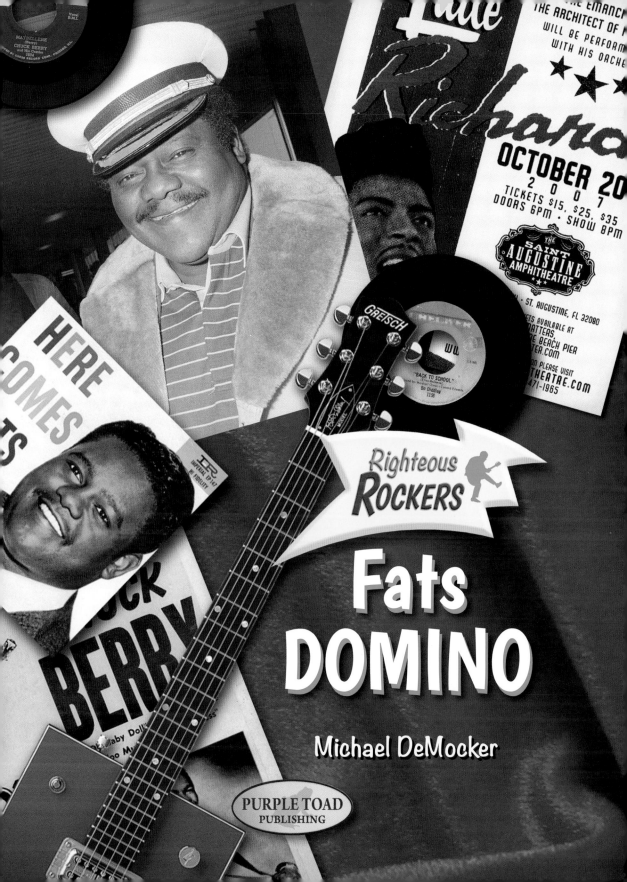

Righteous
ROCKERS

Fats DOMINO

Michael DeMocker

PURPLE TOAD
PUBLISHING

Copyright © 2019 by Purple Toad Publishing, Inc. All rights reserved. No part of this book may be reproduced without written permission from the publisher. Printed and bound in the United States of America.

Printing   1   2   3   4   5   6   7   8   9

PUBLISHER'S NOTE
This series, Righteous Rockers, covers racism in United States history and how it affected professional music. Some of the events told in this series may be disturbing to young readers.

ABOUT THE AUTHOR: Michael DeMocker is an award-winning photojournalist and writer who lives in New Orleans with his wife, son, a tennis ball–obsessed Labrador puppy, and a sarcastic pug. He was lucky enough to be in front of the stage to photograph the final public performance of Fats Domino in 2007.

Publisher's Cataloging-in-Publication Data
DeMocker, Michael.
   Fats Domino / Written by Michael DeMocker.
      p. cm.
Includes bibliographic references, glossary, and index.
ISBN 9781624694103
1. Domino, Fats. 1928-2017 — Juvenile literature. 2. Rythm and blues musicians — United States — Biography — Juvenile literature. 3. Rythm and blues musicians — New Orleans — History — Biography — Juvenile literature. I. Series: Righteous Rockers
 ML420.A45 2019
 782.421
[B]
Library of Congress Control Number: 2018943799
ebook ISBN: 9781624694097

Bo Diddley
by Nicole K. Orr

Chuck Berry
by Wayne L. Wilson

Fats Domino
by Michael DeMocker

Little Richard
by Wayne L. Wilson

Sam Cooke
by Wayne L. Wilson

Contents

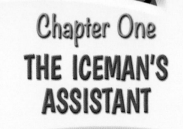

Chapter One
THE ICEMAN'S ASSISTANT

"I've got no time for talkin'
I've got to keep on walkin'
New Orleans is my home
That's the reason why I'm goin'
Yes, I'm walkin' to New Orleans
I'm walkin' to New Orleans"
           —Fats Domino, "Walking to New Orleans"

Though it was still early in the morning, it was already a sweltering day in the city of New Orleans. It was too hot to work, to play, to do much of anything but sit outside with a fan, hoping for a breeze. It was the summer of 1939, and air conditioning and icemakers were still many years from being brought to homes and businesses.

In the Lower Ninth Ward neighborhood, a girl sat outside her family's restaurant, awaiting the cry that would bring them some relief from the sweltering heat.

"Iceman! Iceman!"

The young woman stood as Ed Ridgley came down the street in his ice wagon. Pulled by a mule,

In the days before refrigeration, ice was stored in an icehouse and delivered by wagon to homes by an iceman.

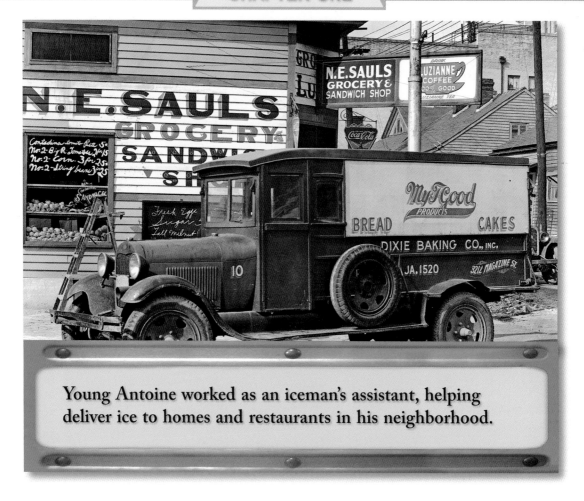

Young Antoine worked as an iceman's assistant, helping deliver ice to homes and restaurants in his neighborhood.

the ice wagon delivered blocks of ice from an icehouse where the ice was stored. When the blind and skinny iceman stopped in front of the girl, a chubby eleven-year-old boy carried a sweating block of ice from the wagon into the restaurant. Mr. Ridgley brought the girl a handful of ice chips, which she used to cool her face and neck.

As the iceman sat next to her to take a break in the shade, the girl heard piano music coming from the restaurant. The family had bought a beat-up piano that her father played for the restaurant's customers when the mood struck him. But this music was different. It was rollicking, energetic, and fun. It made her want to get up and dance— and so, despite the heat, she did. She took Mr. Ridgley's hand and danced with him in the street as the cheerful melody cut through the hot summer morning. Soon the pair was happily sweating as the girl twirled and swayed. Eventually Mr. Ridgley became too tired and sat down, clapping along to the girl's dancing.

When the music stopped, it occurred to the girl she had no idea who had been playing. She ducked her head into the restaurant. Getting up from the piano was the iceman's young assistant, looking a bit guilty, his shirt still wet from the block of ice, his face sweaty from his lively performance. The girl clapped for him, and he smiled shyly. The boy climbed back up on the ice wagon and Mr. Ridgley took the mule's reins to head to the next delivery. As the wagon rolled away, Mr.

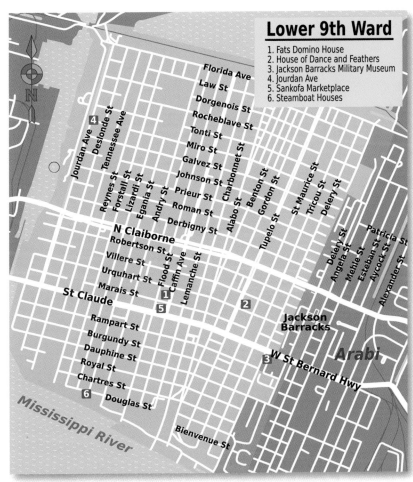

Lower 9th Ward
1. Fats Domino House
2. House of Dance and Feathers
3. Jackson Barracks Military Museum
4. Jourdan Ave
5. Sankofa Marketplace
6. Steamboat Houses

The Lower Ninth Ward is a low-lying neighborhood along the Mississippi River on the southeast side of New Orleans.

Ridgley called back to the girl "Miss, that's Antoine Domino, Jr. He's going to be a big star one day."

The girl watched the mule, the iceman, and the iceman's talented assistant disappear down the street. She thought, "I do believe you are right."

A statue of Fats Domino stands in New Orleans Musical Legends Park in the French Quarter.

NEW ORLEANS

The Louisiana city of New Orleans was founded by Frenchman Jean-Baptiste Le Moyne de Bienville in 1718. In 1763, the city was given to Spain. Forty years later, in 1803, it was returned to France. Just a few weeks later, New Orleans became part of the United States when President Thomas Jefferson made the Louisiana Purchase.

Along with its rich European history, New Orleans is a major port. In its early days, it traded heavily with Caribbean islands and South American countries. New Orleans became a center of diverse musical, architectural, and culinary influences. That is why the food, music, and the city itself are so unique compared to the rest of the United States, and why visitors have flocked to the "Big Easy" for many generations. Many come to hear jazz, the musical style born in the famed French Quarter of New Orleans. This grid of European-style streets lies along the big bend in the Mississippi River. Others come for the city's famous Mardi Gras, the pre-Lenten celebration that features fancy street parades. There, lucky revelers can catch beads, doubloons, or other prizes thrown by a "krewe" of riders. Food lovers also flock to the city for local dishes like red beans and rice, crawfish étouffée, jambalaya, or fried shrimp po'boy sandwiches. Today, New Orleans is home to over 390,000 people. It hosts two professional sports teams: the NFL's New Orleans Saints and the NBA's New Orleans Pelicans.

"The Mardi Gras Indians" parade during the New Orleans Jazz & Heritage Festival.

"You'll see a smiling face,
A fireplace,
A cozy room,
A little nest that's nestled where the roses bloom."
　　　　　—Fats Domino, "My Blue Heaven"

Antoine Domino, Jr., was born on February 26, 1928, to Antoine Domino, a fiddle player, and his wife, Marie-Donatile. Antoine Jr. was the youngest child of the couple's eight children. They lived on Jourdan Avenue in the Lower Ninth Ward neighborhood of New Orleans, Louisiana, a city nicknamed the Big Easy. Antoine Sr.'s parents had been slaves on the Golden Star Plantation in Vacherie, Louisiana.

The main language spoken in the Domino house was not English, but Creole French. This was because the family's ancestors worked in the sugarcane fields west of New Orleans. The region had been settled by French-Canadians, known as Cajuns. The language was a blend of French and assorted African languages. It allowed the African slaves and French-

Antoine "Fats" Domino, Jr., as a young citizen of New Orleans, grew up hearing live music nearly every day of his life.

Fats' grandparents were slaves in the sugarcane fields of Louisiana, They spoke Creole French, a blend of French and African languages that allowed plantation owners and slaves to communicate.

speaking plantation owners to communicate. Fewer than 10,000 people still speak Creole, greeting one another with *"bonjou,"* meaning "hello," or *"Konmen to yê?"* meaning "How are you?"

Looked after by his mother and older sisters, Antoine attended elementary school a few blocks from the family's home. He helped out after school by chopping firewood for the cooking fires. He was a shy boy who liked to box and make extra money collecting scrap metal. He also loved to eat. He remembered when his mother used to cook: "If she happened to turn her back, I'd steal a couple of shrimp when she'd be soaking them for gumbo."[1] Gumbo is a famous Louisiana stew made with vegetables, meat or shellfish, and stock thickened by okra.

Two kinds of cooking are famous in Louisiana: Creole and Cajun. Creole food is an urban style invented in New Orleans. It mixes European, Native American, and African cooking. The gumbo Antoine loved is Creole. So is shrimp étouffée, a blend of shrimp, vegetables, and spices served in a flour-based sauce called a roux (*ROO*). Cajun cuisine combines traditional Southern food with a kind of French cooking brought to Louisiana by French-Canadian immigrants. It usually consists of a meaty mixture served in one big dish. Jambalaya, a mix of meat, spices, and rice, is a classic Cajun dish.

Okra is widely used in Southern cooking and is a key ingredient in gumbo.

New Orleans was a good place for a food lover like Antoine to grow up.

While New Orleans is known for its food, it is also known for its music. Music seems to be everywhere in the Big Easy, from the brass bands marching in Mardi Gras parades to street musicians performing for

A big pot of jambalaya

A marching band performs during a Mardi Gras parade in New Orleans.

tips in the French Quarter. The city's jazz funerals include music and dancing to celebrate the life of the person who died. Children are taught by their older relatives how to play instruments, and families often gather on weekends to play music together at backyard picnics. People born in New Orleans are raised on music.

Antoine was no exception. More than anything, the young Antoine loved music. He listened to swing bands on the family radio and played records on their windup gramophone. On Saturdays, friends and neighbors gathered at the Domino house to play music and to dance. When Antoine was ten, the family bought a well-worn piano for the home. Harrison Verrett, the husband of Antoine's older sister Philonese, was a jazz guitarist. He taught Antoine how to play the family piano, never suspecting he would change musical history.

Antoine played the piano whenever he could. He would copy the songs he heard on the radio and on jukeboxes. He played so much his parents moved the piano to the garage so that they could get some peace from their son's constant playing.[2]

Antoine was especially good at playing "boogie-woogie" piano music, a style of blues music popular at the time. It was developed by African American musicians and featured a more rhythmic, danceable beat than traditional blues music.

Soon, Antoine was performing in his backyard for his neighbors, with his friends and family playing along. To make money as a preteen, he took a job as an iceman's assistant, delivering ice to bars and restaurants. Ice-making machines were not available until the 1950s, so ice had to be delivered from ice warehouses. Antoine often played the piano in the places where he delivered ice. He also worked at the Crescent City Bed Factory, where he would attach springs to bed frames. He suffered an accident while working that nearly cost him the use of one hand, but he recovered and went on to continue playing piano.

Harrison Verrett, who was very close to Antoine, helped give his young brother-in-law the chance to play at the Court of Two Sisters.

New Orleans offered many colorful restaurants and businesses.

Fats Domino's brother-in-law Harrison Verrett helped the young musician get the chance to play at the Court of Two Sisters in the French Quarter.

This popular restaurant was in the French Quarter of New Orleans. Antoine was surprised by how much money people put in his tip jar. He recalled, "I picked up about eight or nine dollars within ten minutes. Oh, man! That was a lot of money."[3] During the 1940s, that amount of money was indeed a lot for a young musician to make in just one turn at the piano. In today's money, that's about $120.[4]

Antoine soon realized that the thing he loved to do best could also be a source of money and maybe even a career. During an era when African Americans were segregated and separated by law from the opportunities of white society, especially in the American South, music was one way for a young black man to provide for himself and his family.

Funerals in New Orleans often feature music, a tradition brought over from Africa. A traditional New Orleans jazz funeral is one of its finest farewells. It begins with a brass band that accompanies the hearse from the church to the cemetery. At first the band plays somber, serious music of mourning, such as the hymn "Just a Closer Walk with Thee." People leave their houses and fall in behind the procession as it makes its way through the streets.

The procession is led by the "first line"—the family, funeral directors, friends, and fellow musicians. The people who follow behind them are the "second line." Often the procession passes through points in the neighborhood that were important to the person, such as his or her home or a club where the person had performed.

After the funeral, or when the body is "cut loose," as people would say, the band strikes up more cheerful tunes, such as "When the Saints Go Marching In." The people in the second line dance and wave handkerchiefs and umbrellas. The sad funeral procession turns into a rowdy, joyful celebration of the life of the deceased. Using dance steps like the "buck jump" and the "high step," dancers fill the streets while others add to the music of the band by blowing whistles, banging tambourines, or making music with whatever is at hand.

Musicians lead a traditional New Orleans jazz funeral.

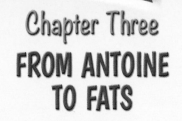

Chapter Three
FROM ANTOINE TO FATS

*"They call, they call me the fat man
'Cause I weigh two hundred pounds
All the girls they love me
'Cause I know my way around."*
—Fats Domino, "The Fat Man"

On a hot summer day in 1947, Antoine and his brother went for a sno-cone, a traditional New Orleans treat of sweet syrup poured over shaved ice and served in a paper cone. The sno-cone stand was owned by the Halls family, who happened to have a piano in their house next door. Antoine could not resist playing a song on the Halls' piano, and the family loved his playing. Antoine, in turn, fell in love with the Halls' teenage daughter Rosemary. Later that summer, the two were married. They would eventually have eight children together, giving them all names that begin with the letter "A": Antoine III, Anatole, Andre, Antonio, Antoinette, Andrea, Anola, and Adonica.

Fats Domino loved kids and often took time to sign autographs for them.

The former J&M Recording Studio, owned by Cosimo Matassa, was at 840 N. Rampart Street on the edge of the French Quarter. It is now a laundromat, although the tiled entrance and a plaque mark the building's place in musical history.

During one of the Domino family's backyard concerts in 1947, local bandleader Billy Diamond heard Antoine perform. He was so impressed, he asked Antoine to play his boogie-woogie piano in his band. Antoine agreed, and Diamond's band soon became the regular house band at the newly opened and very popular Club Desire in the Upper Ninth Ward. The club featured dancers, paintings, and a wondrous new device called a television, which showed programs from New Orleans' single TV station.

Antoine was only five feet four inches tall, and his love of New Orleans food had him sporting extra weight.[1] In 1948, Diamond gave Antoine the nickname that would stick with him the rest of his life: Fats. Diamond wasn't trying to be mean when he gave "Fats" his

Dave Bartholomew

nickname. He believed that the young Antoine would be as famous as two other musicians called Fats: piano players Fats Waller and Fats Pichon.

Around this time, trumpeter Dave Bartholomew had become famous in New Orleans for his up-tempo style of blues music called "jump blues." People would flock to see the famed black bandleader and his suit-and-tie-clad band perform at Al's Starlight Inn on North Dorgenois Street. One night Fats Domino, still in his work clothes, came to listen to the music. When the band stopped playing to take a break, the bar owner told them, "Look, man, if y'all don't play, the people gonna walk out."[2] Bartholomew had seen the young piano player dressed in work clothes and didn't want him to play, but drummer Earl Palmer wanted to give Fats a chance, so Palmer let him take the stage. Fats took to the piano and woke up the room with a couple of rollicking boogie-woogie songs. Little did he know that the popular Dave Bartholomew would help make his a household name.

In 1949, while playing at the Hideaway Club, Fats Domino got his first big break. At the suggestion of Bartholomew, a record producer named Lew Chubbs came to see Fats perform.[3] Years later, Bartholomew talked about Fats' performance at the Hideaway Club that night: "Fats was rocking the joint. And he was sweating and playing, he'd put his whole heart and soul in what he was doing, and the people was crazy about him."[4] Chubbs loved Fats' talent so much, he offered him a recording contract with Imperial Records.

Cosimo Matassa

J&M Recording Studio was owned and run by Cosimo Matassa. At the age of 18, this white former chemistry major left Tulane University to open his own recording business in the back of his family's shop on North Rampart Street. On December 10, 1949, Fats joined Bartholomew and several other musicians at Matassa's studio to record Fats' first record. Bartholomew had reworked a kind of depressing song called "The Junker's Blues," adding happy, new lyrics about watching Creole women as they sashayed past the corner of Rampart and Canal Streets in downtown New Orleans.

On that December day, all the musicians crammed themselves into the tiny recording studio and cut a song called "The Fat Man." Matassa served as the engineer for the session, engraving the music as it was played. Fats played his boogie-woogie piano and belted out a chorus of "wah wah wah" in between singing about being a fat man watching girls pass by.

The session lasted about six hours. The record was produced and sent to stores just before Christmas of 1949. It was an instant success; the song sold around one million records. Not only was it a success in sales, many music historians argue that "The Fat Man" was the world's first rock and roll song.[5]

The success of "The Fat Man" didn't suddenly make the Dominos rich. Fats and his wife still lived with her parents, and he stilled worked at the mattress factory. But Fats Domino's star was on the rise.

After the success of their collaboration for "The Fat Man," he and Bartholomew continued to work together. Bartholomew acted as

A New Orleans streetcar turns off Canal Street onto N. Rampart. The intersection was made famous in Fats Domino's first hit, "The Fat Man."

bandleader, producer, and songwriter for Fats and his band. Over the next few years, they had a string of big hits, including "Ain't That a Shame," "Blueberry Hill," "Blue Monday," and "Walking to New Orleans." With his energetic piano playing mixed with his fun "wah-wah-wah" and "woo-hoo" style of singing, Fats won many fans. He appeared on major television shows to perform his music and was even in movies. He made enough money to move out of his in-laws' house, although he and Rosemary did not go too far: they bought the house next door.

The success of Fats Domino was of course due to his talent, but it was helped by the musical and technological changes that happened after World War II (1941–1945). Young people no longer wanted to hear the big band music their parents listened to, but instead flocked to blues, jazz, and the kind of feel-good boogie-woogie Fats played. Also, music simply became easier to listen to. People no longer had to go to a club or a concert to hear their favorite band or performer.

Fats Domino mixed his energetic piano playing with his fun "wah-wah-wah" and "woo-hoo" style of singing.

Improvements to the phonograph made it possible for the average person to buy and play their own music on vinyl records. In the 1950s, television brought live musical performances into people's living rooms. The widespread availability of Fats Domino's music made his rise to fame faster and easier than it would have been a generation before.

Fats Domino became one of the most successful male rhythm and blues singers of the 1950s. During that decade, he had forty-six songs on the R&B charts, including nine that went to the very top.[6] But what made him even more special was that he appealed to pop music fans as well. Thirty-one of those forty-six songs made it to the pop charts. Placing on both the R&B and the pop charts was truly a key to his success.

Only one singer had more songs on the pop charts during the 1950s: a young man from Tupelo, Mississippi, named Elvis Presley.[7] Elvis also sold the most records in the 1950s, but Fats was right behind him, with 65 million records sold.[8] While other musicians are credited with inventing rock and roll during the 1950s, many music historians agree it was the groundbreaking songs of Fats Domino that ushered in the era of this wildly popular new musical genre.

During an interview in 1956, Fats said, "What they call rock-and-roll is rhythm and blues, and I've been playing it for 15 years in New Orleans."[9]

WHAT IS A RECORD?

Most people today listen to their music digitally, using electronic gadgets such as phones or MP4 players. The music lovers of Fats Domino's generation listened to records on phonographs. Records were made of vinyl and had one long continuous groove etched into it. Sound recordings were inscribed into the groove. A record player's turntable would spin the record, and a sound needle on an arm would ride in the groove, playing the music through a speaker.

People would go to record stores and flip through the selection to decide what to buy, usually after hearing the song played on the radio. Small records were for sale, with one song on each side— usually a hit song on one side and a less popular song on the "B-side." LPs, or long-playing records, contained an entire album (usually 8 to 12 songs). The problem with records was if they got scratched, they were unplayable.

The vinyl record survived some changes in technology, like the cassette tape, but when the compact disc (or CD) came along in the 1980s, the vinyl record lost its edge. In recent years, however, vinyl records have made a comeback. Some people believe that music originally recorded using analog, not digital, methods actually sound better on vinyl.

A vinyl record on a phonograph's turntable.

Chapter Four
MUSIC FOR EVERYBODY

"Saturday mornin', oh Saturday mornin'
All my tiredness has gone away
Got my money and my honey
And I'm out on the stand to play"
—Fats Domino, "Blue Monday"

Fame took Fats Domino all over the world. But no matter where he traveled, he always had New Orleans, and its food, on his mind. While touring, he would carry a supply of red beans, cooking up the New Orleans dish whenever he had a craving.[1] Fats once filled a hotel in Nice, France, with the delicious smell of stewed pigs' feet as he cooked in his room.[2]

A major reason for Fats Domino's success was that his music reached across racial lines, appealing to young white music lovers as well as to African Americans. After World War II, African Americans were still segregated, or separated, in U.S. society. They were forced to sit in the back of buses, banned from lunch counters, required to attend separate schools from whites, and made to listen to music from the balconies at music clubs while white people were given prime spots on the floor.

Even with his fame and popularity, Fats Domino was not allowed in many hotels and restaurants because of the color of his skin.

Fats Domino's music was popular across racial lines, appealing to young white music lovers as well as to African Americans.

It was common in New Orleans for dozens of people to be arrested for "race-mixing" at music clubs for breaking of these "Jim Crow" laws. During the 1950s, Fats Domino would sometimes have to perform two separate shows, one for whites and a second for African Americans.[3] But his shows were so popular, this arrangement could be troublesome.

On May 4, 1956, hundreds of white teenagers went to the African American show in Roanoke, Virginia. During the performance, many of the whites came down from the overcrowded balcony and joined the African American audience on the floor. They sang and danced together until the end of the show, when someone threw a bottle at the mixed-race crowd. A riot ensued, and Fats had to hide under his piano to avoid the projectiles. The venue banned future "race-mixing" shows.

It was by no means the last time fights would break out at one of Fats' concerts. When asked years later why there were so many riots at his concerts, Fats answered, "I don't know. It wasn't anything in the music, so it must have been something in the audience."[4]

Civil rights activists are denied entry into a Florida restaurant in 1961.

On the road, despite his fame, Fats was still turned away from hotels and restaurants and was required to use "For Colored Only" services. Back home in Louisiana, lawmakers continued to enact rules against race mixing. But history was changing, slowly, and the music of Fats Domino continued to find fans across racial lines. Many activists, including Dr. Martin Luther King, Jr., worked toward gaining racial equality in America. Meanwhile Fats' music was already bringing people together. A writer at the time commented that his music was "doing a job in the Deep South that even the U.S. Supreme Court hasn't been able to accomplish with its groundbreaking 1954 decision outlawing school segregation."[5]

Fats was popular not just across racial lines; he also had admirers from other countries. Some of his biggest fans were the Beatles. This

The Beatles arrive in America in 1964, home of their idols Buddy Holly, Chuck Berry, Elvis Presley, Carl Perkins, and Fats Domino.

British band put 65 songs on the pop charts during their stellar career.

As successful as the Beatles were, Fats Domino put more songs on the pop charts than the young men from Liverpool. Fats had 66 songs make it to the pop charts during his career.[6]

George Harrison of the Beatles says Fats' "I'm in Love Again" was the first rock-and-roll song he'd ever heard.[7] The first song John Lennon said he learned to play was Fats' "Ain't That a Shame," a

George Harrison

song Paul McCartney has called one of his top ten favorites of all time.[8] In 1964, before the Beatles performed at Tad Gormley Stadium in New Orleans' City Park, they got together with Fats backstage. Together, they sang Fats' "I'm in Love Again." When asked many years later if he got to meet the Beatles when they came to New Orleans, Fats replied, "No, they got to meet me."[9]

Lennon and McCartney wrote the song "Lady Madonna" as a tribute to Fats Domino.[10] In a 1994 interview, McCartney said, " 'Lady Madonna' was me sitting down at the piano trying to write a bluesy boogie-woogie thing. . . . It reminded me of Fats Domino for some reason, so I started singing a Fats Domino impression. It took my other voice to a very odd place."[11] Fats recorded his own version of "Lady Madonna" in 1968. That version became the last Top 100 song in his marvelous career.

By the time his recording career ended,

From left to right: Ringo Starr, George Harrison, John Lennon, and Paul McCartney, in the film *Magical Mystery Tour*. They would record "Lady Madonna" soon after.

Fats had sold 110 million records and earned 23 gold records. In 1985, after a series of performances and videos, Fats decided he was going to return to New Orleans for good. He moved back and vowed never to leave, saying he was tired of all the travel. He also said he couldn't find food on the road as good as the food they had in New Orleans.[12]

He did make one special trip out of town. In 1986, the Rock & Roll Hall of Fame opened in Cleveland, Ohio. For his lifetime of accomplishments, Antoine "Fats" Domino was voted in with the very first class of musicians to be inducted.

At the end of his recording career, Fats had sold 110 million records and earned 23 gold records. In 1986, he was inducted into the Rock & Roll Hall of Fame.

JIM CROW LAWS AND MUSICIANS

After the Civil War (1861–1865), state and local governments in America's southern states sought to keep African Americans from mixing with white society. Called Jim Crow Laws, these rules kept African Americans from using the same public transportation, public schools, restaurants, hotels, restrooms, and even drinking fountains as whites.

Jim Crow laws affected musicians as well. Blacks and whites were not allowed to mix at concerts, for example. The whites could be on the floor, while the black concertgoers had to watch from the balcony, even if the performer on stage was African American. Jim Crow laws also said that blacks and whites could not be in bands together. In many places, including New Orleans, this rule was often ignored, and people would be arrested. In a February 1949 raid of a French Quarter club, 65 people were arrested for "race-mixing." While kept "separate but equal" in the outside world, blacks and whites in the music clubs of New Orleans shared common ground in their love for music, and this opened a window of tolerance. The Civil Rights Act of 1964 eventually did away with the Jim Crow laws. It outlawed segregation and granted equal rights to all citizens regardless of race, religion, sex, or national origin.

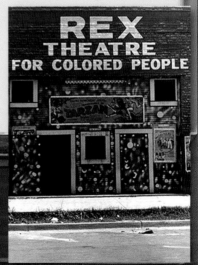

Under the discriminatory Jim Crow laws, blacks and whites were prohibited from "race mixing" at music venues.

Chapter Five
THE HURRICANE AND AFTER

*"All over the country, people wanna know
What ever happened to Fats Domino?
And I'm alive and kickin'
I'm alive and kickin'
I'm alive and kickin'
And I'm where I wanna be."*

—Fats Domino, "Alive and Kickin' "

In August 2005, a tropical storm formed in the Atlantic Ocean. It quickly gathered strength and moved into the Gulf of Mexico, where the Mississippi River empties after it passes New Orleans. The warm waters of the Gulf fed the storm, and it became the dangerous Hurricane Katrina.

New Orleans has a long history of hurricanes. In 1965, Hurricane Betsy struck, flooding Fats' Lower Ninth Ward neighborhood with seven feet of water. Fats lost many possessions, including instruments and cars, when the floodwaters reached his family's home. Hurricane Katrina was poised to strike even harder than Betsy.

The storm surge from Hurricane Katrina pushed ships, like this cargo ship and four fishing boats, far up onto land.

A rescue helicopter flies over a New Orleans neighborhood flooded by Hurricane Katrina.

Despite calls to evacuate, Fats and his family chose to ride out the hurricane in their home. In the early morning hours of August 29, Hurricane Katrina roared ashore. As the Domino family sheltered in the house, a barge broke loose in the nearby Industrial Canal. The barge smashed through a retaining wall that was already stressed from the storm surge. Water began to pour into the Lower Ninth Ward. Fats, his wife, five children, and other family members made their way to the second floor as nine feet of water rushed into their home.

In the days that followed, concerned people from across the country, knowing Fats had stayed home during the hurricane, began to fear the worst: that Fats Domino and his family were among the over 1,800 people who had died in the storm.

But soon word arrived that they were safe. Around 9:00 p.m. on the night of the storm, a rescue boat had found the family and plucked them from danger. Fats and his family ended up in Baton Rouge, the capital of Louisiana, about eighty miles northwest of New Orleans. There, they stayed for a time with JaMarcus Russell, the quarterback for the Louisiana State University football team who was dating one of Fats' granddaughters.

On October 15, 2005, Fats returned to his flooded home in the Lower Ninth Ward. Someone who thought he had died had left a painted sign above his porch. It read, "R.I.P. FATS . . . YOU WILL BE MISSED."

Someone who thought Fats had died in Hurricane Katrina left a message on his house in the Lower Ninth Ward.

One of Fats Domino's pianos, a 1980s-era Steinway baby grand, was recovered from his flooded home following Hurricane Katrina. It is now on display at the Presbytére museum in New Orleans.

When he went into the damaged house, Fats discovered that only three of his 23 gold records remained—for "Rose Mary," "I'm Walkin'," and "Blue Monday."[1] A framed picture of him with Elvis Presley was damaged beyond repair. He lost two pianos as well, including a magnificent white Steinway grand piano that had been the centerpiece of his living room.

That piano had soaked in the floodwaters for many days. It was eventually salvaged by the Louisiana State Museum. The museum raised $35,000 to restore it to its former glory. Today, it is on display at the museum in the French Quarter.

On May 19, 2007, Fats returned to the stage for a special concert at the famed Tipitina's music hall in New Orleans. Many feared he would not perform again. He had canceled his appearance at the 2006 New Orleans Jazz & Heritage Festival—his first scheduled appearance since the storm—just hours before he was to go on. Some say he canceled because of the nervousness he had battled all his life. But take the stage at Tipitina's he did, performing several of his hits, and then slipping away after thirty minutes. It was Fats Domino's last public performance.

The following August, two years after Katrina struck, the Recording Industry Association of America held a special ceremony in which the twenty gold records Fats had lost were replaced. Still shy despite decades of performing, Fats told the gathered crowd, "There ain't too much I can say but thanks. Thank you very much."[2]

The gold records weren't the musician's only awards lost in Hurricane Katrina. Also gone was the National Medal of Arts presented to Fats in 1998 by then-President Bill Clinton. The medal is the highest honor the United States government gives to artists and musicians. President George W. Bush came to the Dominos' home in the Lower Ninth Ward to replace the medal.

Fats enjoyed his retirement in a suburb of New Orleans. His longtime home and office in the Lower Ninth Ward was restored and

In the aftermath of Hurricane Katrina, President George W. Bush replaced Fats' National Medal of Arts lost in the storm.

The musical legend died at home on October 24, 2017 at the age of 89.

is a popular photo opportunity for passing tourists. When asked if he wanted to return to his Lower Ninth Ward home, he replied, "I hope so. I like it down there."[3]

Sadly, it was not to be. Antoine "Fats" Domino died peacefully on October 24, 2017, at the age of 89, surrounded by his family.

The following week, on November 1, All Saints Day, people from all over the city, people of all ages and colors, gathered for a traditional New Orleans jazz funeral to bid farewell to their native son. People wore blue clothes in honor of his songs "Blue Monday" and "Blueberry Hill." As the marchers made their way through the neighborhood, more and more people came out of their homes and businesses to join in. A truck rode along with the parade, blasting Fats Domino songs.

Famous New Orleans entertainers mixed with regular folks, dancing to the music of a brass band as they second-lined under the setting sun. It was a fitting final tribute to the iceman's young assistant from the Lower Ninth Ward, the grandson of slaves, the legendary musician who helped usher in the modern era of rock and roll.

HURRICANE KATRINA

In late August 2005, Tropical Storm Katrina struck Florida and moved into the Gulf of Mexico. Once over the warm water of the Gulf, the storm quickly strengthened to become a Category 5 hurricane, the most powerful kind of hurricane. Despite weakening to a Category 3, Katrina slammed into the Gulf Coast. The storm was an estimated 400 miles wide with winds between 100 and 140 miles per hour. Its eyewall, or center, came ashore at Gulfport, Mississippi, where the damage was catastrophic.

Much of the city of New Orleans is below sea level. A system of levees, or walls, protects it from the sea. However, many of these were poorly maintained, and they were unable to handle the wind and heavy rain of Hurricane Katrina. As the storm struck New Orleans on the morning of Monday, August 29, storm surge caused the levees to fail in over fifty places. Floodwaters covered 80 percent of the city. In some places, including the Lower Ninth Ward, it was 14 feet deep. Those who were able scrambled to the roofs of their homes and hoped for rescue by boat or helicopter.

When the disaster was over, an estimated 1,833 people had died, 1,400 of them just in New Orleans. It took many years for former residents to return to the city, and many never did. While many houses in the Lower Ninth Ward have been rebuilt and the Industrial Canal wall repaired, there are still a great number of empty lots where homes used to stand, a reminder even many years later of the destruction Hurricane Katrina brought to the neighborhood.

A satellite photo shows the massive Hurricane Katrina as it approaches New Orleans and the Gulf Coast in 2005.

1928   Antoine Domino, Jr. is born in New Orleans on February 26.

1938   The Domino family buys a piano. Antoine's brother-in-law Harrison Verrett teaches him to play.

1947   Bandleader Billy Diamond hears Antoine perform at one of the family's backyard concerts and invites him to play his boogie-woogie music at the Hideaway Club. Antoine marries Rosemary Hall on August 6.

1948   Diamond nicknames Antoine "Fats."

1949   Fats Domino records "The Fat Man," what many call the first rock and roll song, on December 10.

1955   In August, Fats Domino records "Ain't That a Shame." In November, he releases his debut album, *Carry On Rockin'*.

1956   In September, Fats Domino records "Blueberry Hill." Two months later, he appears on *The Ed Sullivan Show*.

1957   Fats Domino records "I'm Walkin'."

1960   He records "Walking to New Orleans." Six-year-old Ruby Bridges becomes the first African American to integrate an all-white southern school when she attends William Frantz Elementary School near the Domino family home.

1964   In July, President Lyndon B. Johnson outlaws Jim Crow laws when he signs the Civil Rights Act. This law is designed to end discrimination in public places based on race, sex, religion, or national origin. In September, Fats Domino and the Beatles meet backstage at the Beatles' concert in New Orleans.

1965   Hurricane Betsy pounds New Orleans.

1986   Antoine "Fats" Domino is one of the first inductees into the Rock & Roll Hall of Fame.

1998   President Bill Clinton presents Fats Domino with the National Medal of Arts.

2005   On August 29, Hurricane Katrina strikes New Orleans, flooding the Dominos' home in the Lower Ninth Ward.

2007   Fats Domino makes his last public performance at Tipitina's music club in New Orleans. The Recording Industry Association of America replaces the gold records he lost to Katrina.

2008   Fats Domino's wife, Rosemary, dies on March 10 in New Orleans.

2017   Antoine "Fats" Domino dies on October 24 at his home in a New Orleans suburb.

2018   Jon Batiste and Gary Clark Jr. perform a tribute to Fats Domino and fellow rock-and-roll pioneer Chuck Berry during the Grammy awards.

Chapter 2: Born in the Big Easy

1 Coleman, Rick. *Blue Monday: Fats Domino and the Lost Dawn of Rock 'n' Roll*. Cambridge, MA: Da Capo Press, 2006, p. 18.
2 Ibid., p. 20.
3 Ibid., p. 22.
4 Bureau of Labor Statistics. "CPI Inflation Calculator." United States Department of Labor, 2017. www.bls. gov/data/inflation_calculator.htm.

Chapter 3: From Antoine to Fats

1 "Before Elvis, Jerry Lee, and Chuck Berry, There Was Fats." Rock & Roll Hall of Fame, 2017. www.rockhall. com/inductees/fats-domino
2 Coleman, Rick. *Blue Monday: Fats Domino and the Lost Dawn of Rock 'n' Roll*. Cambridge, MA: Da Capo Press, 2006, p. 27.
3 Aswell, Tom. *Louisiana Rocks!* Gretna, LA: Pelican Publishing, 2010, p. 51.
4 Thompkins, Gwen. "Fats Domino, Architect of Rock 'n' Roll, Dead At 89." NPR, October 25, 2017. www.npr. org/sections/thetwo-way/2017/10/25/522583856/fats-domino-architect-of-rock-and-roll-dead-at-89
5 Aswell, p. 13.
6 Ibid.
7 Ibid.
8 Ibid.
9 Pope, John. "Fats Domino, Piano-Playing Prodigy and Rock and Roll Legend, Dies at 89." NOLA.com, October 25, 2017. www.nola.com/music/index.ssf/2017/10/fats_domino_dies.html.

Chapter 4: Music for Everybody

1 McCash, Doug. "Fats Domino: Recalling the Diamonds, Red Beans, and Rock 'n' Roll." NOLA.com, October 25, 2017. www.nola.com/music/index.ssf/2017/10/fats_domino_quint_davis_marcia.html
2 Ibid.
3 Coleman, Rick. *Blue Monday: Fats Domino and the Lost Dawn of Rock 'n' Roll*. Cambridge, MA: Da Capo Press, 2006, p. 122.
4 Young, Charles M. "Fats Domino, Big Easy Legend, Hits New York." *Rolling Stone*, December 13, 2007. http://www.rollingstone.com/music/features/fats-domino-still-cooks-20071213.
5 McCash.
6 Aswell, Tom. *Louisiana Rocks!* Gretna, LA: Pelican Publishing, 2010, p. 50.
7 Ibid., p. 53.
8 Ibid.
9 Scott, Mike. "The Beatles and the Fat Man: The Story behind the Photo." NOLA.com. October 25, 2017. www.nola.com/music/index.ssf/2016/09/the_beatles_and_fats_domino.html.
10 Aswell, p. 53.
11 Marinucci, Steve. "Fats Domino and The Beatles Were Mutually Fond of Each Other." AXS, October 26, 2017. www.axs.com/fats-domino-and-the-beatles-were-mutually-fond-of-each-other-124633.
12 Aswell, p. 53.

Chapter 5: The Hurricane and After

1 Aswell, Tom. *Louisiana Rocks!* Gretna, LA: Pelican Publishing, 2010, p. 54.
2 Spera, Keith. "Fats Domino Holds His Gold Records Once Again." NOLA.com, August 23, 2007. http://blog. nola.com/living/2007/08/fats_domino_holds_his_gold_rec.html
3 Mitchell, Mary Niall. "The Piano That Can't Play a Tune." *The Atlantic*, August 26, 2015. http://www. theatlantic.com/politics/archive/2015/08/fats-dominos-white-piano/401552/

Works Consulted

Aswell, Tom. *Louisiana Rocks!* Gretna, LA: Pelican Publishing, 2010.

Bureau of Labor Statistics. "CPI Inflation Calculator." United States Department of Labor, 2017. Accessed October 2017. www.bls.gov/data/inflation_calculator.htm

Coleman, Rick. *Blue Monday: Fats Domino and the Lost Dawn of Rock 'n' Roll.* Cambridge, MA: Da Capo Press, 2006.

Doyle, Patrick. "Inside Rock Legend Fats Domino's World: Crawfish, Cards, Boogie Woogie." *Rolling Stone*, February 26, 2016. Accessed October 2017. www.rollingstone. com/music/news/inside-rock-legend-fats-dominos-world-crawfish-cards-boogie-woogie-20160226

Hannusch, Jefferey. *The Soul of New Orleans: A Legacy of Rhythm and Blues.* Ville Platte, LA: Swallow Publications, 2001.

Marinucci, Steve. "Fats Domino and The Beatles Were Mutually Fond of Each Other." AXS, October 26, 2017. Accessed October 2017. www.axs.com/ fats-domino-and-the-beatles-were-mutually-fond-of-each-other-124633

McCash, Doug. "Fats Domino: Recalling the Diamonds, Red Beans, and Rock 'n' Roll." NOLA.com, October 25, 2017. Accessed October 2017. www.nola.com/music/index. ssf/2017/10/fats_domino_quint_davis_marcia.html

McCash, Doug. "Fats Domino Second-Line Parade Rambles into the 9th Ward Night." NOLA.com, November 1, 2017. Accessed October 2017. www.nola.com/music/index. ssf/2017/11/fats_domino_second-line_parade.html

Mitchell, Mary Niall. "The Piano That Can't Play a Tune." *The Atlantic*, August 26, 2015. Accessed October 2017. www.theatlantic.com/politics/archive/2015/08/ fats-dominos-white-piano/401552/

PBS. "Fats Domino and the Birth of Rock 'n' Roll." PBS, January 8, 2016. Accessed October 2017. www.pbs.org/wnet/americanmasters/fats-domino-and-the-birth-of-rock-n-roll/6230/

Pope, John. "Fats Domino, Piano-Playing Prodigy and Rock and Roll Legend, Dies at 89." NOLA.com October 25, 2017. Accessed October 2017. www.nola.com/music/index. ssf/2017/10/fats_domino_dies.html

Reuters. "Fats Domino Returns Home to New Orleans." *Today Show*, October 15, 2005. Accessed October 2017. https://www.today.com/popculture/ fats-domino-returns-home-new-orleans-wbna9711008

Rock & Roll Hall of Fame. "Before Elvis, Jerry Lee, and Chuck Berry, There Was Fats." Rock & Roll Hall of Fame, 2017. Accessed October 2017. www.rockhall.com/inductees/fats-domino

Rolling Stone. "Fats Domino Bio." *Rolling Stone*, 2017. Accessed October 2017. www.rollingstone.com/music/artists/fats-domino/biography.

Saslow, Eli. "Music Legend 'Fats' Domino Coping With Katrina." *Washington Post*, September 2, 2005. Accessed October 2017. www.washingtonpost.com/wpdyn/content/article/2005/09/02/AR2005090201578.html

Sakakeeny, Matt. "Jazz Funerals and Second Line Parades." *Encyclopedia of Louisiana*. Louisiana Endowment for the Humanities, October 2, 2017. Accessed February 4, 2018. http://www.knowlouisiana.org/entry/jazz-funerals-and-second-line-parades

Scott, Mike. "The Beatles and the Fat Man: The Story Behind the Photo" NOLA.com, October 25, 2017. www.nola.com/music/index.ssf/2016/09/the_beatles_and_fats_domino.html

Siegel, Robert. "Fats Domino, 'Alive and Kickin' After Katrina." NPR, March 13, 2006. Accessed October 2017. www.npr.org/2006/03/13/5259801/fats-domino-alive-and-kickin-after-katrina

Spera, Keith. "Fats Domino Holds His Gold Records Once Again." NOLA.com, August 13, 2007. Accessed October 2017. http://blog.nola.com/living/2007/08/fats_domino_holds_his_gold_rec.html

Spera, Keith. "Reclusive Fats Domino Takes the Tipitina's Stage to Prove He Still is the King of 'Blueberry Hill.'" NOLA.com, May 23, 2007. Accessed October 2017. www.nola.com/music/index.ssf/2007/05/reclusive_fats_domino_takes_th.html

Thompkins, Gwen. "Fats Domino, Architect of Rock 'n' Roll, Dead at 89." NPR, October 25, 2017. Accessed October 2017. www.npr.org/sections/thetwo-way/2017/10/25/522583856/fats-domino-architect-of-rock-and-roll-dead-at-89

Young, Charles M. "Fats Domino, Big Easy Legend, Hits New York." *Rolling Stone*, December 13, 2007. Accessed October 2017. www.rollingstone.com/music/features/fats-domino-still-cooks-20071213

On the Internet

Fats Domino Official Website.
www.fatsdominoofficial.com

analog (AN-uh-log)—Not involving or using computer technology.

architectural (ar-kih-TEK-shur-al)—Having to do with the design of buildings.

Cajun (KAY-jun)—Any of the French-Canadian people who settled in parts of Louisiana; the culture of the Cajuns.

catastrophic (kat-ah-STROF-ik)—Causing great destruction and loss of life.

Creole (KREE-ohl)—The language of the Cajun people.

culinary (KUH-lih-nayr-ee)—Having to do with cooking or the kitchen.

discrimination (dis-krih-mih-NAY-shun)—Unjust or unfair treatment of people based on their race, age, gender or sexual preference.

doubloon (dub-LOON)—An old Spanish gold coin.

étouffée (ay-too-FAY)—A Cajun dish of seafood or chicken served over rice.

gramophone (GRAM-uh-fohn)—An early form of record player.

induct (in-DUKT)—To admit as a member.

integrate (IN-teh-grayt)—To mix together.

jambalaya (jahm-buh-LY-uh)—A hot dish of meat, spices, and rice.

Jim Crow—Laws and traditions that kept black people from mixing with whites, especially in public places.

Mardi Gras (MAR-dee GRAW)—Meaning "Fat Tuesday," a day of celebration held just before the first day of Lent, a 40-day period when many Christians do not eat certain foods or enjoy certain activities as a way to remember how Jesus suffered.

okra (OH-kruh)—A peppery vegetable with thick, sticky juice that is used to thicken stews.

rollicking (RAH-lih-king)—Joyful or high-spirited.

sashay (saa-SHAY)—To strut or walk with grace.

segregate (SEH-greh-gayt)—To separate according to color or race.

PHOTO CREDITS: Cover, pp. 11, 24, 28—Hugo Van Gelderen; p . 1—Bart Molendkij; p. 3—Rudi Mental; p. 5—Russell Lee; p. 6—Walker Evans; p. 7—Peter Fitzgerald; pp. 8, 9, 14, 15, 20, 23, 38—Michael DeMocker; p. 37—Infrogmation; pp. 30, 33, 35, 36—Public Domain; p. 12—Queensland Archives; p. 13—Annie, AFL-CIO; p. 17—Daniel X. Oniel; p. 21—Klaus Hiltscher; p. 22—WhyArts; p. 24—Jamelle Dolphin; p. 25—Blue Breeze; p. 27—Richard Proctor; p. 29—Florida Memory Project; p. 30—Steve Mathieson; p. 31—Parlophone Music Sweden; p. 32—Rob Cicroes; p. 39—Eric Draper; p. 40—Ronzoni; p. 41—NASA. Every measure has been taken to find all copyright holders of material used in this book. In the event any mistakes or omissions have happened within, attempts to correct them will be made in future editions of the book.

Harris County Public Library
Houston, Texas